D0435198

Once Upon a Princess

Adapted by Lisa Marsoli • Based on the movie *Once Upon a Princess*, written by Craig Gerber
Illustrated by Character Building Studio and the Disney Storybook Artists

Sofia's Special Day

A Royal Wedding Scrapbook

Written by the Disney Book Group • Based on the movie *Once Upon a Princess*, written by Craig Gerber
Illustrated by Character Building Studio and the Disney Storybook Artists

Copyright © 2013 Disney Enterprises, Inc. All rights reserved. Published by Disney Press, an imprint of Disney Book Group.
No part of this book may be reproduced or transmitted in any form or by any means, electronic or mechanical, including
photocopying, recording, or by any information storage and retrieval system, without written permission from the publisher.
For information address Disney Press, 1101 Flower Street, Glendale, California 91201.

ISBN 978-1-4231-4656-8
G942-9090-6-13249
Manufactured in the United States of America

For more Disney Press fun, visit www.disneybooks.com

Disney PRESS
New York • Los Angeles

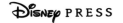

SUSTAINABLE FORESTRY INITIATIVE   Certified Sourcing
www.sfiprogram.org
SFI-00993
This Label Applies to Text Stock Only

Once upon a time, in the kingdom of Enchancia, there lived a little girl named Sofia. She and her mother, Miranda, didn't have much but their cobbler shop, but they were happy.

One morning, Sofia and her mother went to the castle to bring King Roland a new pair of shoes. He and Miranda took one look at each other, and it was love at first sight.

The couple married, and soon Sofia and her mom were off to the castle for a life they never could have imagined.

Miranda lovingly greeted the king's children, Princess Amber and Prince James. King Roland placed a tiara on Sofia's head. "Welcome to the family!" he said warmly.

At dinner that evening, Sofia counted six different forks by her plate! Silverware clattered to the floor as she picked up one fork, then another.

King Roland could see it was going to take a while for Sofia to get used to her new royal life. He had a surprise to help her feel welcome. "We will be throwing a royal ball in your honor at week's end," he said. "And you and I shall dance the first waltz."

Later in Sofia's mom's room, Sofia said, "I don't know how to be a princess. And I don't know how to dance."

Miranda smiled down at Sofia and assured her daughter she'd be fine if she just tried her best.

Just then, they heard a knock at the door.

It was King Roland—with a beautiful gift for Sofia!

"It's a very special amulet," he told her. "So you must promise to never take it off. Now you best run off to bed. You have princess school in the morning."

Princess school! Sofia liked the sound of that.

As Sofia skipped back to her room, she bumped into Cedric. The royal sorcerer's beady eyes spotted the amulet. It was the Amulet of Avalor—the powerful charm Cedric had been trying to get for years! With its magic, he could rule Enchancia. Cedric began to scheme how he'd trick Sofia into giving it to him.

The next morning, the headmistresses of Royal Prep Academy—Flora, Fauna, and Merryweather—greeted Sofia at the Academy gates.

Sofia's classmates liked her a lot—which made Amber jealous. She was used to being the popular one!

Amber turned to James. "I think it's time Sofia took a ride on the magic swing."

So James led Sofia to the swing. "Try it! It swings itself."
Sofia climbed onto the swing. The swing suddenly sped up
and sent her flying into the fountain! Sofia put on a brave
smile while the other kids laughed, but James could tell she
was upset. He felt terrible about tricking his new sister.

Sofia hurried off to dry her dress. As she tried to hold back her tears, she heard frantic chirping. A baby bird had fallen out of its nest! As she gently placed the tiny thing next to its mother, the amulet around her neck began to glow. "There you go," Sofia said to the birds.

When Sofia turned to leave, she thought she heard a tiny, squeaky voice say "Thank you." But she must have been hearing things. Birds didn't talk!

When Sofia arrived home, Cedric was waiting. "How would you like a private tour of my lair—I mean, workshop?" he asked Sofia.

In Cedric's workshop, Sofia saw a picture of the Amulet of Avalor. "That looks just like my amulet!" she said.

"The Amulet of Avalor contains powerful magic. I can take a quick look at your amulet," Cedric said slyly.

Sofia shook her head. "I promised never to take it off."

As soon as Cedric saw his plan wasn't working, he rushed her out the door. This was going to be tougher than he thought.

The next morning, Sofia awoke to find Clover, a rabbit, and his bird friends Robin and Mia on her bed. Sofia could understand every word they were saying! The amulet gave Sofia the power to talk to animals!

After breakfast with her new friends, Sofia left for Royal Prep. She hoped her second day would be better!

Sofia tried hard in all her classes, but she went home feeling discouraged again. "I thought being a princess would be easy," she sighed to her mother. "But it's really hard."

Miranda had a surprise. Sofia's two best friends, Jade and Ruby, were waiting at a fancy table set for tea!

James joined the party, too. He still felt bad about tricking Sofia and wanted to make it up to her.

Soon Sofia was curtsying and pouring tea like a proper princess, but she told James she still didn't know how to dance.

"No problem," he assured her. "We have dance class with Professor Popov tomorrow."

Amber had been watching everyone have fun without her. Now she was even more jealous of her stepsister. She had to make sure Sofia didn't dance better than she did!

The next day, before dance class, Amber gave Sofia a sparkling pair of dance slippers to wear.

Sofia put on the slippers, which immediately took control of her feet. She spun helplessly across the floor, and collapsed into a pile of pillows.

"Oh, Sofia! I must have grabbed a pair of Cedric's trick shoes by mistake. Sorry about that," Amber said with a smile.

Sofia decided she couldn't chance another disaster at the
ball. When she got home, she went straight to Cedric for help.
He gave Sofia a magic spell to say when the waltz began. Little
did she know that the spell would put everyone to sleep and
then Cedric could steal the amulet!

Soon it was time for the ball. James came into Amber's room.
"You gave Sofia the trick shoes on purpose," he said angrily.
"You're trying to ruin her ball because everyone likes her more
than you. And after what you did today, so do I!"

"James! Come back!" Amber called. She ran after him—and
accidentally tore her gown! How could she go to the ball now?

Sofia stood in front of her own mirror and stared at herself in her fancy gown and glittering tiara. She felt like a real princess!

For the first time that week, Sofia was actually looking forward to the ball!

King Roland proudly escorted a beaming Sofia into the ballroom.
It was time for the first waltz!

Sofia confidently spoke the magic words Cedric had given her:
"Somnibus populi cella."

Everyone instantly fell asleep—including Cedric!

"I said it wrong!" Sofia cried as she ran from the ballroom. Sofia sank to the floor and cried. A single tear fell onto her amulet and made it glow. Suddenly, a blue light appeared— and transformed into Cinderella!

"Your amulet links all the princesses that ever were," Cinderella said. "When one of us is in trouble, another will come to help. Why are you so sad, Sofia?"

Sofia told Cinderella about trying to use a magic spell to help her become a better princess.

Cinderella smiled as she explained that she hadn't always been a princess, either. But she discovered that the people who truly cared about you didn't care which fork you used or how well you danced.

Cinderella couldn't undo the spell, but she suggested that Sofia
try to become true sisters with Amber—something she'd never been
able to do with her own stepsisters. "Perhaps all Amber needs is a
second chance," Cinderella said. Then she disappeared!

Sofia went to Amber's room and told Amber about the spell. When Amber saw her father in the ballroom, she gasped in shock!

Sofia felt terrible. "It's all my fault," she said sadly.

Amber shook her head. "No, Sofia," she said. "You wouldn't have needed the spell if I didn't give you those trick shoes."

The girls realized that what they really needed was each other.

Together they went to Cedric's workshop to find a spell to wake everyone up. Clover, Mia, and Robin locked Cedric's pet raven, Wormwood, in his cage.

Clover tricked Wormwood into revealing where the counterspell book was hidden. Wormwood didn't realize that with her amulet, Sofia could understand every word he said. Now Cedric's spell could be broken!

Sofia and Amber were rushing to the ballroom when Amber remembered her torn dress. "I can't go in there!" she cried.

But Sofia wasn't about to leave her sister behind. She quickly mended the gown. "Good as new!" she said.

Now it was Amber's turn to help. She led her sister in a waltz until Sofia was ready for the ball.

Sofia smiled as she took her place beside the king and read the counterspell aloud. "Populi cella excitate!" Everyone woke up.

Cedric was furious that his plan had been ruined! He flicked his wand and disappeared in a puff of smoke. "Merlin's mushrooms!" he yelled.

Meanwhile, Sofia and the king began to waltz.

Sofia looked up at her new dad. "I've been wondering. Why do they call you Roland the Second?" she asked.

"My father was also named Roland," the king explained.

"So I guess that makes me Sofia the First," Sofia said, smiling.

And it was plain to see that this princess was going to live happily ever after!

Amber James Dad Mom Me

That special day was just the beginning of my new life as **Princess Sofia the First!**

That was the day we became **a family.**

The honour of your presence is requested at the royal wedding of MIRANDA OF DUNWIDDIE and KING ROLAND II of Enchancia at the Enchancia Castle

I think the wedding cake was taller than me! And it tasted yummy!

Then there was a huge feast. I had never seen so much delicious food in all my life!

The royal musicians played beautiful music and everyone danced.

Mom and King Roland promised to love each other forever.

A royal coach came to take my mom and me to the castle for the wedding.

I couldn't believe that the castle was going to be my new home. It was enormous!

Amber and I were flower girls in the ceremony. We walked down the aisle in front of my mom and tossed flower petals along the way.

This is the day I met the king for the very first time. My mom was fitting him for new slippers.

It was love at first sight! The king asked my mom to marry him, and she said yes!

Not only did I get a new dad, but I got a new sister and a brother, too!

Princess Amber

Prince James

Best friends forever!

This is Ruby and Jade. They are my best friends.

Here I am in front of our old house in the village.